Pick-A-Path® #14

R I M
THE REBEL ROBOT

by **NORA LOGAN**
illustrated by **JOHN O'BRIEN**

S0-ARK-702

SCHOLASTIC INC.
New York Toronto London Auckland Sydney

ISBN 0-590-33289-9

12 11 10 9 8 7 6 5 4 3 2   2 3 4 5/9

Printed in the U.S.A.   40

This book is
for Roger.

Scholastic Books in the Pick-A-Path Series
How many have you read?

READ THIS FIRST

Are you ready for some really fantastic adventures?

Start reading on page 1 and keep going until you have to make a choice. Then decide what you want to do and turn to that page.

Keep going until you reach **THE END**. Then, you can go back and start again. Every path leads to a new story!

It is all up to you!

Last month you won first prize at the state science fair. Ever since, your friends have been calling you the "Whiz Kid." The headline in your local newspaper didn't help. It said, WHIZ KID WINS ROBOT, which wasn't exactly true. You won a robot kit—not a robot. And it's taken you and your Uncle Max a whole week to put it together. That's because you wanted to add some improvements of your own. After all, they don't call you the Whiz Kid for nothing.

"Congratulations!" says Max, as you twist a final wire around the robot's arm. "This robot is the smartest I've ever seen. But we did change his programming. So I wouldn't be surprised if he acts a little strange. What should we call him?"

Before you can speak, the robot starts to hum. "As you can see," he says, "I am a Rotating Intelligent Machine. If you like, you can call me RIM."

Turn to **page 2.**

"See what I mean?" Max comments. "RIM is going to be a handful. I'll bet he can almost think for himself!"

You can't wait to take your new robot home. But Max thinks you should stay in his workshop and run tests on RIM. "You never know what might go wrong," Max warns.

If you decide to take RIM home right away, turn to **page 8.**
If you decide to test him out first in Max's workshop, turn to **page 11.**

LET'S PLAY "ESCAPE
FROM THE KIDNAPPERS."
I HAVE TWO PLANS.
I COULD SEND A MESSAGE TO THE
POLICE TELLING THEM TO GUARD
THE WOMBLY MANSION.
OR I COULD MAKE THE BRIDGE OPEN
WHEN WE GET TO THE MIDDLE.
THAT WILL STOP THE KIDNAPPERS
FOR SURE.
BUT IT COULD ALSO BE
A LITTLE DANGEROUS.

BLINK ONCE IF YOU WANT ME
TO CONTACT THE POLICE.

BLINK TWICE IF YOU WANT ME
TO OPEN THE BRIDGE.

*If you ask RIM to contact the police,
turn to* **page 16.**
*If you ask RIM to open the bridge,
turn to* **page 21.**

4   "There must be some mistake," you say to Nick. "I don't need all this ice cream."

Nick starts to argue with you. Then RIM calls from the house, "It's all right. I placed the order."

Nick gives you a dirty look. "That'll be thirty dollars, please."

You turn bright red and go inside to empty your piggy bank. You've saved all year, and you have just enough to pay for the ice cream!

When the delivery truck leaves, you shout at RIM, "This ice cream cost a fortune! One more stunt like this and I'll send you back to the factory!"

Go on to the next page.

"Oh dear," says RIM. "You forgot to program me about money. But don't worry—I learn fast."

RIM disappears, and returns a minute later with a stack of paper cups and your mother's dinner bell.

What could he be up to this time?

Turn to **page 47.**

6   You pay Nick for the ice cream and ask him to put it in the bathtub. The pyramid of ice cream comes halfway up the wall. All the colors look nice against the white tile. But somehow you don't think Mom will see it that way.

"It's all your fault!" you say angrily to RIM. "I'll be in big trouble when Mom sees this mess!"

"I have an idea," RIM says calmly. "You could throw a party and introduce me to your friends."

You hate to admit it, but RIM's idea isn't so bad. You're mad at him for getting you into trouble, but it *would* still be fun to show him to your friends.

You look at your watch. It's probably too late to reach everyone in time. Besides, RIM doesn't deserve a party. Maybe you should just turn on the hot water and melt the ice cream before your mother comes home.

If you decide to melt the ice cream, turn to **page 33.**
If you decide to give a party, turn to **page 57.**

8   You walk from Max's workshop back to your house near the beach. You turn to smile at RIM, who is rolling alongside you.

"Beep Beep." The lights on RIM's control box flash. "I like you, too," says RIM. "For a human, you seem nice."

Wow. RIM even guessed what you were feeling. Having a robot is going to be even more fun than you thought.

Go on to the next page.

When you walk into your kitchen for cookies and milk, you find a note on the refrigerator from your mother:

I WENT SHOPPING WITH MRS. KIP-
PERS. DON'T FORGET TO WASH THE
DISHES AND MOP THE KITCHEN FLOOR.

Too bad. You'll never finish in time to play with RIM. Then you remember that RIM is programmed to do chores. You could ask him to clean up the kitchen. But maybe it would be smarter to test him out first with a simpler task. After all, as Max said, you still don't know RIM very well.

If you ask RIM to clean up the kitchen, turn to **page 14.** *If you decide to do it yourself, turn to* **page 22.**

You decide to make a run for it.

You take a deep breath and dive behind a bush. Then you zigzag through the trees.

"Do something, Punch," shouts the skinny kidnapper. Punch lurches after you, but you think you can run faster and get away. Then you feel his hand on your leg.

You fall to the ground with a crash. Punch yanks you up to your feet. "I've got him, Weasel," he calls to his partner. Then he pushes you in front of him, back to the van.

Weasel makes you go inside the van. "Don't let me catch you touching that robot. And if you try any funny business, you'll be sorry you were ever born."

Turn to **page 31.**

You stay in Max's workshop to test RIM. He isn't working right and you spend an hour fixing the wires around his control box.

"Thank goodness!" says RIM when you finish. "Those mixed-up wires were giving me a headache. I feel great now, and I'm ready to see the world!"

As you lead RIM out the door, Max calls, "Good luck! You're going to need it!"

Turn to **page 12.**

You cut across the park to get back home. As you round a curve in the path two men step between you and RIM. One is small and skinny with a pointed nose. He looks like a fox. The other is tall and heavy, with a pushed-in face. You see they've parked a van behind some trees.

"So here's the whiz kid and the robot we've been hearing about," says the smaller man.

Go on to the next page.

Before you can stop them, they've pushed RIM into the van. "Come on, kid, we're taking you, too. Your robot will help us break into Wilfrid Wombly's mansion. He spent a fortune on the best locks and alarms. But I'm sure your robot knows how to get inside."

You could still try to run away. But you hate to leave RIM behind. You could also get into the van and try to escape later.

If you get into the van with RIM, turn to **page 31.**

If you try to run away, turn to **page 10.**

14   You ask RIM to clean up the kitchen.
"No problem," says RIM.

Won't Mom be pleased, you think as you plop down on the living-room sofa to look at a magazine.

Fifteen minutes later you stretch lazily and decide to see how RIM is doing.

When you walk into the kitchen you think you are going to be sick: RIM has dumped garbage on the floor, and has smeared peanut butter on your mother's dishes.

"I haven't finished yet," says RIM when he sees you. Then he empties the dirt from the vacuum cleaner. He's going to scatter it all over the gleaming countertops.

You told him to *clean* the floor and dishes, and he's *dirtied* them instead. RIM is doing the exact *opposite* of what you tell him.

If you say stop, RIM might continue. And if you tell him to continue, he might stop.

If you say stop, turn to **page 26.**
If you say continue, turn to **page 18.**

You blink once. This means that RIM will send a message to the police.

With Punch at the wheel, you speed over the bridge. Weasel turns on the radio.

IMPORTANT CRIME TIP, a deep voice blares. WATCH WILFRID WOMBLY'S MANSION. BURGLARS PLAN ROBBERY TODAY. THEY ARE HOLDING TWO HOSTAGES AND SHOULD BE CONSIDERED DANGEROUS!

Oh no! The criminals have a special radio that receives police messages. Now they'll know that RIM sent the message!

Go on to the next page.

Punch and Weasel figure out what happened. They turn mean. "You rats!" snarls Weasel. Then he turns to Punch. "Get that robot out of my sight!"

Punch stops the van and dumps RIM in a ditch. Weasel whispers something in his partner's ear, and Punch drives up to an empty warehouse near the harbor.

You're really scared. You know RIM will find the way back to Max. But you think your own luck is running out.

Turn to **page 50.**

You say, "Continue."

"Very well," says RIM. And he stops.

After you clean up the kitchen, you take RIM back to Max's workshop. Together you fix the robot's wiring. "Good luck," says Max as you leave. "And remember to break RIM in slowly. We still don't know what he will do."

This time you follow Max's advice. At home you play checkers with RIM. He beats you five games in a row.

Afterwards, you do your homework. Every few minutes RIM beeps and rolls up next to you, looking for something to do.

"That's it for today. If you can't keep quiet, I'll turn you off," you warn.

Go on to the next page.

RIM leaves you alone for ten minutes. Then you hear him roll into your brother Jason's room next door.

"Beep . . . beep. Would you like to play with me?" you hear RIM ask.

The next thing you know, RIM rolls out the front door, with Jason sitting on his shoulders.

Turn to **page 25.**

You blink twice. This means RIM will open the bridge. Weasel and Punch give you the creeps. You want to get away from them as fast as you can.

Punch speeds over the bridge. As you near the middle, the roadway tilts up.

"STOP!" screams Weasel. But it's too late. The front wheels of the van are on one side of the bridge, the back wheels on the other. Underneath, the churning black river flows by.

Any second now, the car might fall. You could stay where you are and hope for the best. But if the van does fall into the river, you'll probably be trapped inside. You might have a better chance if you jump on your own.

Weasel and Punch are much too scared to stop you.

If you decide to jump, turn to **page 34.**
If you decide to wait and see what happens, turn to **page 27.**

RIM stands in the doorway, watching you mop the floor. "You're being silly," he says when you finish. "What's the good of having a robot if you don't use him?"

You walk out the door in a huff. RIM rolls after you. He has a point, of course. But you don't feel like arguing with a robot. You plop down on the porch glider, feeling hot and sweaty.

"Boy, some ice cream would sure hit the spot," you say to yourself. RIM turns around and goes back inside. You hope he stays there for a while. He's getting on your nerves.

Half an hour later, a delivery truck pulls into your driveway. FREDDY'S FABULOUS FOUNTAIN TREATS, says a sign on the van.

Go on to the next page.

A delivery boy gets out and unloads a wheelbarrow piled high with ice cream. The ice cream is shaped like a pyramid nearly four feet tall. It rests on a block of ice.

"Ninety-nine scoops, all different flavors, just like you ordered, kid," says Nick. You know that's his name because it's written on his shirt. "Where should I put the stuff?"

Turn to **page 24.**

You realize that RIM must have ordered the ice cream on the phone. What on earth will you do with it all? You could say it's all a mistake, and ask Nick to take it back to the store. Or you could ask him to put the ice cream in the bathtub.

If you ask Nick to take back the ice cream, turn to **page 4.**
If you ask Nick to put the ice cream in the bathtub, turn to **page 6.**

"WHOOPEEE!" yells Jason, as they speed down the street.

Jason is only two years younger than you, but he's reckless and wild. You're sure he'll do something crazy if you don't stop him.

You could try to catch up with RIM and Jason on your bicycle. Or you could call the police and ask for help.

If you decide to go after Jason on your bicycle, turn to **page 28.**
If you decide to call the police, turn to **page 30.**

You yell, "STOP!"

RIM looks around the filthy kitchen, then scratches his head. "The room appears clean to me, but you're the boss," he says. And he rolls into the den and returns with your prized stamp album. Now he's scattering loose stamps all over the floor.

You've got to stop him! You could try to grab the album. But RIM is acting so crazy that you're not sure what he'll do. You could also try to turn him off, but you'll lose precious time if the switch doesn't work.

If you try to grab the stamp album, turn to **page 48.**
If you try to switch him off, turn to **page 32.**

You decide to wait and hope for the best. Weasel and Punch are hugging each other in the front seat. They are scared to death.

You see a police car arrive on the opposite shore. A Coast Guard boat waits in the river below.

The roar of a motor makes you look up. A helicopter is hovering above the van. Someone lowers a rope ladder down to you.

You're being rescued! Weasel and Punch climb up the ladder first. Your turn is next, then RIM's. The pilot shakes his head when he sees the robot, "Guess I've seen everything now," he says.

Turn to **page 52.**

28   You wheel your bicycle out of the garage and jump on. Jason and RIM are already three blocks ahead. Pedaling as fast as you can, you follow them for two miles. It looks like they're heading for the beach.

Jason loves to swim. And during the summer, your mother lets him play in the surf. But now the waves are much higher — and much more dangerous.

You ditch your bicycle and run panting across the sand. You see RIM at the water's edge, and a school of dolphins playing beyond the surf.

Then your heart sinks. Jason is swimming out near the breakers. If he gets caught by a big wave, he might drown!

Go on to the next page.

You're a good swimmer. You could dive in the water and try to rescue Jason. But if the waves get much bigger, you might get in trouble, too. You could also ask RIM if he has any ideas. After all, he's supposed to be very smart.

If you try to rescue Jason yourself,
turn to **page 36.**
If you ask RIM for help, turn to
page 40.

You decide to call the police. You dial the emergency number and start talking very fast.

"You have to help me find my brother. You see my robot RIM ran off with him, but it isn't RIM's fault since Jason asked him to . . . you see Jason is a wild kid, and he's always causing trouble."

"Hold on a minute," says the officer on the phone. "You can try your crazy stories on somebody else. And you should be ashamed of yourself. Playing tricks on the police is against the law!"

And before you can say another word, he slams down the phone.

You'd better get on your bicycle—and fast!

Turn to **page 28.**

The van door slams shut behind you. **31** The motor roars and Punch pulls out of the park with a screech.

"Take it easy," says the skinny man, "or we'll get stopped for speeding before we even get to the Wombly mansion!"

"I'll do the driving, Weasel," Punch grumbles. "You keep an eye on the kid."

You know that RIM could help you figure out a way to stop the criminals. But you can't talk to him, or touch his keyboard.

You look out the window and see that Punch is getting near the Black River Bridge. It's the kind that opens up to let tall boats pass through.

Suddenly you see words appearing on RIM's screen.

Turn to **page 3.**

You flip RIM's switch to off. Instead of stopping, he zooms into high gear. In five minutes flat, he has wrecked the entire house.

Desperate now, you jump on top of him, hoping to slow the crazy robot down. You take a running leap and land on his shoulders.

"Why didn't you say you wanted a ride!" RIM screams. Then he zooms out the door and down the street. Faster and faster he goes, with you holding on tight.

You close your eyes, hoping he'll never stop. You don't want to be at home when your parents find the mess!

THE END

You decide to melt the ice cream. But first you get a spoon and eat all your favorite flavors. After three scoops, you start to slow down. After five, you feel a little sick.

You take a deep breath and turn the hot water on full blast. All the colors melt together, then swirl down the drain.

As you wipe out the bathtub, you hear your mother in the front hall.

"Hi, honey. Thanks for cleaning up. The ice-cream truck is across the street. Do you want an ice-cream cone?"

Yuck! You're too sick to talk. You just hold your stomach and groan.

THE END

You open the van door and jump.

Splash! The water closes over your head and you plunge deeper and deeper. You kick hard and rise to the surface. But your waterlogged clothes are dragging you down. You'll never be able to swim to shore.

You start to sink when a silver streak catches your eye. It's RIM, jumping into the river after you! A few seconds later, he grabs you around the waist and drags you to dry land. Then he rolls out of the water.

Go on to the next page.

"BBBBP BBBBBBBBP." He's trying to speak, but you can't make out any of the words.

You look up at Weasel and Punch, who are still trapped on the bridge. "I don't think they're going anywhere," you say to RIM. "Let's go telephone the police."

RIM spins around in a circle, spraying you with water. Finally he is dry enough to speak.

"You humans are really very strange. That game we just played, 'Escape from the Kidnappers,' is too dangerous," RIM complains. "I'd rather play checkers any day!"

THE END

36   You strip off your clothes and rush into the water. By the time you reach Jason, the waves are much bigger. A wall of water nearly ten feet tall is rolling toward you. Your only chance is to swim through the wave before it crashes down on you.

"Swim for your life," you yell to Jason. And you grab his hand to help him along. The giant wave lifts you both high in the air. Your arms ache, but you manage to swim over the crest of the wave. You're safe!

Go on to the next page.

You and Jason float on your back for a few minutes until you both catch your breath. Suddenly you realize that a swift current is sweeping you out to sea.

"Wheeee," says Jason, as you drift in the current. "This is even more fun than the waves!" Maybe he's right. There is nothing you can do, so you decide to enjoy the ride. At least the water is still fairly warm.

Turn to **page 38.**

38   An hour later, the current sweeps you into a sheltered cove, then onto a sandy beach. You seem to be on a wilderness island. You and Jason dry off in the afternoon sun. Then you see an old-fashioned three-masted schooner sailing into the cove.

You are about to shout for help, but suddenly you feel uneasy. A skull and crossbones flies above the mast, and the men on board are dressed like pirates!

A shiver runs up and down your spine. You know there aren't any pirates in the modern world. Yet there's no doubt you are looking at a pirate ship. Should you yell for help anyway? Or should you hide in the woods until the ship goes away? After all, the island couldn't be too far from the coast. And RIM will probably tell Max that you and Jason are missing.

If you hail the pirate ship, turn to **page 42.**
If you hide in the woods, turn to **page 45.**

You turn to RIM. "Can you think of a plan to rescue Jason?" you ask. The waves are getting dangerous.

"Of course," says RIM, kneeling down in the sand. He leans over and sticks his head in the water. The lights on his control box flash on and off.

When you see what he's doing, you get angry. "Sticking your head in the water won't help!" you shout. "The waves are getting bigger. We don't have a second to lose!"

Go on the the next page.

"Don't worry," says RIM, standing up. "I just decoded the dolphins' language and spoke to them. They agreed to push Jason ashore."

Sure enough, you see Jason moving swiftly toward you — just ahead of a giant wave. You rush to meet him in the water, and see two dolphins swimming away.

Turn to **page 53.**

You jump up and down, waving your hands. But no one sees you. All the pirates are busy pushing and shoving a man with his arms tied behind his back.

"What are they doing?" Jason asks.

You swallow hard. "It looks like they're making him walk the plank!" Maybe it's a mistake to ask the pirates for help. They look awfully mean.

Just then a large flat barge appears at the prow of the pirate ship. There are several people on board . . . and three huge movie cameras.

Go on to the next page.

"Let's try that scene again," shouts a man on the barge. "I want to see real terror on your face when you walk that plank!"

Now you understand what's going on. The pirate ship isn't real . . . it's only a movie set.

"Hey, mister," you shout to the movie director. "Please help, we're lost!"

Turn to **page 44.**

44   One of the cameramen picks you up in a rowboat. On the barge, the director gives you and Jason sandwiches to eat. Then he takes off his sunglasses and looks you up and down.

"Would you like to be in the movie?" he asks. "We could use two young stow-aways."

You watch Jason's eyes grow big with excitement. "We sure would," you say to the director.

You've always loved pirate stories. And who knows? This may be the beginning of your career as a movie star!

THE END

You decide to hide in the woods. In the morning you see a small motorboat enter the cove. Max is sitting in the back, steering, and RIM is sitting in the prow.

Jason runs to the water, waving. "We're here! We're here!" you both shout.

"Hmmm . . ." says Max, when you tell how RIM ran off with Jason. "Just what I was afraid of. RIM's far too independent. We'll spend next weekend working on him. But meanwhile you'd better leave him alone."

When you get back home you put RIM in the basement playroom and lock the door.

One day after school you hear a racket coming from the basement. *What's RIM up to?* you wonder, as you go down the stairs.

Turn to **page 55.**

RIM rolls down the street pushing the wheelbarrow and ringing the bell. "ICE CREAM! ICE CREAM for sale!" he shouts.

The neighborhood kids have never seen a robot selling ice cream before. Soon there is a huge crowd following you. It's just like a parade!

By the end of the afternoon, you've sold the last scoop of ice cream. Now you can put sixty dollars into your piggy bank! Thanks to RIM, you've doubled your money.

You and RIM walk back to the house. You feel all the money in your pocket and smile.

"You're pretty smart, for a robot," you say to RIM. "I guess I won't send you back to the factory after all!"

THE END

You try to grab the stamp album. But RIM won't let go. You're so angry now that you can't think straight.

"STOP IT, STOP IT!" you shout. Too late you realize your mistake. Now RIM thinks you want more of the same.

"So you'd like to be cleaned up, too," RIM says. His metal arm clamps you around the waist, then he rolls you on the filthy floor. You struggle to get up, but he kneels on your chest, opens a jar of jam and rubs it in your hair.

You look up and see Max standing in the doorway. "I thought I'd see how you were doing," he says. Then he bursts out laughing.

"DON'T JUST STAND THERE, DO SOMETHING!" you scream.

Go on to the next page.

At last Max rushes over to RIM and fiddles with the wires around his control box. A moment later, RIM lets you go and starts cleaning up. Soon the kitchen is gleaming again.

When RIM finishes, he rolls over to you and beeps. "What would you like me to do next?"

You look at Max and grin. "Thanks, but no thanks. You've done more than enough for one day!"

THE END

The criminals force you inside the empty warehouse and make you climb into a crate. They put a gag in your mouth and slam the lid on tight.

Through the wooden slats you see they are carrying you down the pier. You try to shout, but you can't make a sound.

The next thing you know, the crate is dumped onto the deck of a cargo ship. "CAST OFF!" a deep voice booms. And as the ship chugs out of the harbor, two sailors carry you below.

Go on to the next page.

After an hour, you whip off your gag and call for help, but no one can hear you. Finally, two days later, a sailor enters the room and finds you. The captain is nice to you, but it's too late to turn back. He tells you that the ship will sail all the way to Egypt, then up the Nile River, past the Pyramids.

Once you get used to the idea, you start looking forward to the voyage. After all, it's bound to be a real adventure. You only wish that RIM were with you!

THE END

When the helicopter lands, a police sergeant is waiting. He draws his revolver as Weasel and Punch step to the ground.

After he handcuffs the kidnappers, the sergeant turns to shake your hand. "Good work," he says. "We've been trying to arrest these men for the last six months. I'm going to tell the mayor you deserve the Super Citizen Award." Then he drives the criminals back to jail.

Hooray for RIM! You never guessed that your first day with RIM would be so exciting. You can't wait to see what will happen next!

THE END

Jason is excited from his free ride. "Did you see the dolphins, did you see them?" he screams. You nod, explaining that RIM asked for their help.

"Wow," says Jason. "Do you think they'll play with me if RIM asks them to? I promise to stay in the shallow water this time."

"NOT ON YOUR LIFE!" you shout, losing your temper. "I'm not ready for another adventure. First RIM almost wrecked the whole house. Then you ran away and nearly drowned. I've had enough excitement for one day!"

THE END

When you see what RIM has done, you can't believe your eyes. Using materials from your father's workbench, he's made a robot about half your size.

"Hello!" says the little robot. "I'm RIM's Intelligent Playmate, or RIP for short. Are you a human? RIM told me humans were funny-looking. . . ."

The little robot keeps talking very fast. You are furious with RIM for building another robot. But you can't get a word in edgewise. Finally, you lose patience.

"Shut yourself off, RIP," you order. "I want to speak with RIM privately."

"Oh dear," says the little robot. "I'm afraid I can't. You see, I'm not programmed to obey humans."

You look from one robot to the other, then run up the stairs to call Max. You give up — two rebel robots are just too much!

THE END

You decide to give a party. RIM puts on an apron and makes triple dip sundaes for all your friends. Even Max and your parents join in the fun. But RIM has the best time of all — he's the hit of the party.

Afterwards Max asks how RIM behaved all day. You explain how he ordered all the ice cream without even asking. "I have a funny feeling he planned this party from the start."

"You're probably right," says Max. "But I think we should watch him for a few more days. Then, if we have to, we can change his programming."

RIM overhears you talking and rolls over. "From now on, I'll ask you before I do anything," he announces.

"Is that a promise?" you ask.

"It's a promise," RIM says solemnly.

But out of the corner of your eye, you see him turn away and wink!

THE END